THE

Valentine

MURDER

THE
Valentine
MURDER

PENELOPE LOVELETTER

LOVELETTER
PUBLICATIONS

EST. 2023

Original Text by Penelope Loveletter
Cover design by Penelope Loveletter

Copyright 2025, Penelope Loveletter

All rights reserved. No part of this publication may be reproduced, stored in a retrieval system, or transmitted, in any form or by any means, electronic, mechanical, photocopying, recording or otherwise, without the prior written permission of the publisher and copyright owner.

Other Books by
Penelope Loveletter

♡

The Agatha & Christie Cozy Mysteries:
The Snow Globe Murder
The Valentine Murder

Whispering Pines Cozy Mysteries:
Whispers of Murder
Whispers of Death
Whispers of Mystery
Whispers in the Dark
Macarons and Murder
Meringues and Murder
Mint Tea and Murder

Whispering Pines Sweet Romances:
Whispers by the Lake
Whispers of the Heart
Whispers of Forever

Dedicated to Alan
My Valentine
Forever

♡

Chapter 1

Rose lined up the postcards on her kitchen counter, each one a memory from a place she'd never visited. The weathered edges and faded postmarks adorned Venice's canals, Paris's cobblestone streets, the rolling hills of Tuscany, sunny shores of Puerto Rico, and the jungled hills of Vietnam. She adjusted them within the double-sided glass frame she'd ordered online last weekend, making sure each was perfectly aligned. With glass on both sides, she could turn the frame over and still read the handwritten notes on the backs of the postcards without taking them out. It was the perfect way to preserve them while still being able to read them.

"What do you think, Christie?" She glanced down at her cream point Ragdoll cat, who lay curled in an unusually tight ball on her favorite cushion. "Hmm. Are you still not feeling any better?"

Christie's ears twitched but she didn't lift her head. Rose's heart squeezed. After cleaning up the mess from Christie's breakfast incident, she'd been watching her cat like a hawk. Usually Christie would be prowling the counters by now, especially with the smell of chocolate chip cookies baking in the oven.

Rose secured the back of the frame and lifted it against the wall between her spice rack and the window. "A little to the left, maybe?" She adjusted it until the evening light caught the glossy surfaces just right. The collection of exotic scenes added a splash of color to her cream-colored kitchen walls, although the cards still gave her a pang of sadness.

She stepped back and caught her reflection in the glass. Her shoulder-length dark brown curls had escaped their clips, and she tucked them back in place. At thirty-four, she was aware that she was no longer going to be mistaken for a teen and was also mature enough to be happy about it. She pinched her cheeks and straightened her sweater feeling a flutter as she thought about Jack's response that he'd love to come for a neighborhood game night and would get back in touch to let her know for sure if he could make it.

The timer chimed and Rose jumped. She slipped on her oven mitts and pulled out the last batch of cookies, the warm scent of butter and vanilla filling the air. Steam rose from the golden-brown edges as she transferred them to the cooling rack beside the earlier batches.

Rose's kitchen was in the back of her bookstore, The Literary Cat, that had opened just last month after she'd moved to Whispering Pines from St. Paul. The front of her shop consisted of several rooms of books, complete with a cozy fireplace and comfy armchairs tucked into quiet nooks. Upstairs was her apartment space, with her bedroom and living room. At first, she'd thought it might be inconvenient to have her kitchen downstairs with the bookshop, but tonight she realized it was the perfect layout. It allowed her to entertain in a space that was part bookshop, part home.

She checked her phone. Still no confirmation from Jack. She sighed as Christie let out a pitiful meow.

"I know you're not feeling well, sweet girl. Come on. You'll be more comfortable upstairs." Rose crouched beside Christie's cushion. "We can't have you getting sick during game night."

Christie blinked slowly, her blue eyes glazed. Rose ran her fingers through the soft fur, checking for any unusual warmth or lumps. Nothing seemed out of place, but Christie's lethargy worried her.

She gathered Christie in her arms, the cat limp as the rag dolls her breed was named for, and carried her upstairs to the bedroom. Agatha was already there, sprawled across Rose's pillow in a patch of evening sunlight. Rose settled Christie into her plush cat bed by the window.

"Keep an eye on your sister for me?" Rose scratched behind Agatha's ears. The larger Ragdoll stretched and yawned, showing off her pink tongue.

Back in the kitchen, Rose arranged the cookies on her grandmother's blue and white platter. The frame of postcards caught her eye again and she sighed. Maybe hanging them up wasn't such a good idea. But there was no time to rearrange now.

She filled Christie's water bowl and walked back upstairs to place it beside the cat bed. "Try to drink a little if you can, sweetie." Christie lifted her head slightly, sniffed Rose's hand, then curled up tighter.

Rose glanced at her phone one more time before setting out the plates and napkins. Still no messages from Jack. She'd left the invitation casual - just mentioned game night was happening if he wanted to stop by. Maybe that had been too vague.

The doorbell at the front of her bookstore chimed and Betty Wilson, the elderly president of Whispering Pine's Gardening Society, swept in, a designer handbag swinging from her arm. "I brought my famous lemon bars." She set an elegantly arranged platter on the counter. "And I hope you appreciate them! It was difficult to bake this afternoon. Beverly's been absolutely miserable today, poor dear. Wouldn't touch her breakfast and I was beside myself caring for her all day."

"Christie's been sick too," Rose said, arranging chairs around her oak dining table. "She threw up this morning." It hadn't been Rose's intention to invite Betty to game night, but Betty had overheard her inviting Abigail and had insisted on coming. It was just like her.

"There must be something going around." Betty pulled out her phone and showed Rose a photo of Beverly curled up in her plush dog bed. "Look at her sad little face. I almost canceled tonight to stay with her, but Doctor Hilton assured me she just needs rest. And I'd promised you I'd be here."

Rose's mouth quirked up at this. "I hope Beverly has a peaceful evening." At the mention of Jack Hilton, the town vet, and she pulled out her phone again to check for a reply.

The bell rang again, and she looked up, hopeful.

Rose's friend, Bridget, bounced in, dark curls escaping from a messy bun. She carried a white bakery box tied with Northern Pines Bakery's signature pink ribbon. "Emma sent these specially! They're her new raspberry chocolate cupcakes."

"How sweet of her." Rose peeked in the box at the perfectly frosted treats. "How are the wedding plans coming along? And how are classes?"

"My classes are great! This semester is a pretty easy one. And Daniel bought her the most gorgeous bouquet yesterday - pink roses and white lilies. You should have seen her face light up when he brought them to the bakery."

Isabella Chang, who worked at Whispering Pines' Community Bank and was an avid reader of romantic comedies, arrived next carrying a vegetable platter. "I'm sorry I didn't bake anything," she said, setting the veggies beside Betty's lemon bars. "I just got off work and grabbed these on my way over. I hope that's ok."

"Are you kidding?" Rose popped a carrot stick into her mouth. "After all these cookies, this is exactly what we need."

The door opened again, bringing a blast of February air along with Abigail, owner of the soap shop next door. She was followed by Izzy, the town librarian, and her boyfriend Ethan who carried in a cheese and cracker platter arranged in an artistic spiral.

"The winter festival committee meeting ran late," Izzy said, unwinding her scarf as the door opened again admitting Harrison Cole, the town doctor. "You won't believe what they're planning this year."

"What who is planning?" Harrison asked.

Rose kept one eye on the door as she helped everyone get settled with drinks and snacks. Still no Jack. Maybe he'd just been being polite when he'd love to come.

"Did you hear they're adding an ice sculpture contest?" Ethan asked, dealing cards for the first round of Clue. "Right next to the skating rink."

"Oh yes," Betty said, studying her cards. "And the historical society is organizing horse-drawn sleigh rides around the lake. Of course, the Gardening Society will have our annual winter flower display." She sighed. "But I can hardly keep my mind on it. Did I mention that Beverly's been under the weather today?"

"Christie's been sick too," Rose said, laying down a card. "I've got her quarantined upstairs with Agatha."

"There's been a stomach bug going around the pets," Harrison nodded. "But thankfully it doesn't seem to be bothering the owners."

As the evening progressed, Rose found herself glancing at her phone less and less. They moved from Clue to Uno to Scrabble, and Isabella proved to have an impressive vocabulary. The cookies, cupcakes, and vegetables disappeared quickly.

"These cupcakes are divine," Izzy declared, licking frosting from her fingers. "Emma's really outdone herself."

"Speaking of Emma," Betty leaned forward conspiratorially. "Did you hear that Charlie and Aidan are expecting?"

Bridget looked confused. "What does that have to do with Emma?"

"Well, young couples. Babies." Betty waved her hand. "It's all very exciting."

Rose placed her tiles on the Scrabble board, spelling out "QUIXOTIC" across a triple word score and Betty clapped her hands. Rose smiled to herself and thought that maybe Betty wasn't quite as difficult as her first impression had suggested. She tried not to feel disappointed that Jack hadn't shown up or even sent a message. It wasn't like he'd actually promised to come.

Outside, snow began to fall, dusting the windowsills with fresh powder.

The brass knocker on the front door of The Literary Cat echoed through the closed bookstore. Rose set down her Scrabble tiles and peered through the darkened shop toward the entrance. Through the glass panes, a figure stood silhouetted against the streetlight.

As she pushed back her chair, a plaintive meow drew her attention. Agatha's paw reached under the gap to the door to Rose's upstairs apartment.

"Coming, coming." Rose opened the stairs door first, and Agatha trotted down into the bookstore, her tail held high making Rose smile as she ran a hand over the fluffy cat.

The knocker sounded again, and Rose hurried across the bookshop and unlocked the front door.

A young woman Rose didn't know stood on the stoop, snowflakes dusting her blonde hair. Her eyes were rimmed in red.

"Megan!" Bridget called from the kitchen. "Hey you!"

"I'm so sorry to come by after hours." Megan wrapped her arms around herself. "I just got off work and-"

Rose stepped back to let her in. "You just got off this hour?"

Before she could answer, Bridget hurried out into the bookshop, hugging the young woman and motioning her to come to the back of the house, where games were spread out on the large table. "I heard about your engagement to Mike! Congratulations!" Rose noted that Bridget and this young woman were about the same age and wondered if Megan was in college with Bridget.

"Thanks." Megan smiled as she stepped into the kitchen, but it didn't reach her eyes.

Rose felt a pang as she watched Megan twist her new engagement ring. Would Rose ever find someone to share her life with? She pushed the thought away and focused on helping her customer. "So are you in school too, or do you work somewhere that keeps you late?" Rose said with a kind smile.

"Megan is a hygienist at the dental clinic," Bridget said.

Megan turned to Rose. "I'm sorry for barging in. I just wondered if you happen to have a travel guide for southeast Asia. I'm especially interested in Vietnam, Cambodia and Laos."

"I'm sorry, I don't have any Southeast Asia guides in stock right now. But I can order you one - it should arrive in a couple days."

"That would be great." Megan's voice cracked as she tried to smile.

"Are you alright?" Rose asked softly.

Tears welled in Megan's eyes, and she shook her head. "I'm sorry." She waved a hand as if trying to magic her tears away. "My dog died yesterday."

A collective gasp went up from the game table.

"Mocha?" Betty clutched her chest. "No! What happened? Was she sick?" Her voice rose. "Oh my gosh. Beverly has been sick too!"

Agatha wound between Megan's legs, batting at something pink stuck to the young woman's jeans. Rose scooped up her cat before she could make more mischief.

"Were you at the elementary school today too?" Abigail asked, nodding at the bits of paper. "I was helping the kids make Valentine's Day bath bombs for their moms. It was such a happy mess with all that pink paper flying around."

Megan looked down at the bits of pink paper clinging to one leg of her scrubs. "Oh. Yes." She blinked and wiped her cheeks. "At the school."

"But Mocha!" Betty said, her chair scraping the floor as she turned to Megan. "What happened?"

Megan shook her head. "She got sick, and before I knew how serious it was, I thought it was just a virus or something. But yesterday when I came home for lunch, she was just…" She stopped talking and put a hand to her mouth, shaking her head.

"I am so sorry." Rose offered the young woman a quick hug. "I can't even imagine. Would you like to join us?" She gestured to the game table. "We have an empty spot since one of the people I invited hasn't shown up. It might cheer you up?"

"No, I..." Megan backed toward the door. "I should go. Sorry. I'm pretty shaken up about Mocha. Thanks for ordering the book."

She stepped into the night and the door closed behind her with a soft click.

"Poor thing," Betty said, rearranging her Scrabble tiles. "She's clearly devastated about Mocha. That little dog was everything to her. She got her right after her mother passed away, and I don't think anyone in this town was more devoted to a pet than Megan was to that little fluff ball."

Abigail looked like she was trying to suppress a smile when she said, "That's saying something, Betty, coming from you."

Betty only raised her eyebrows. "As a devoted pet owner, I recognize a true bond when I see one."

Rose settled back at the table with Agatha curled in her lap and pulled out her phone to place an order for a southeast Asian travel guide before she forgot. There were three good ones, and uncertain which Megan would prefer, she ordered all three.

"If anyone ever hurt my sweetie pug, Beverly, I think I'd kill them." Betty shook her head as she rolled the dice. "But I will say, devoted dog owner or not, I'd have thought Megan would have more sense than to get engaged to Mike Cooper."

Rose looked up from her phone. "What do you mean?"

"Oh, Betty. Let's not gossip," Bridget said, arranging her game pieces.

"It's not gossip if it's true!" Betty's lips pressed into a thin line. "That man convinced me to invest in a line of premium dog toys he was developing. Took my money and I haven't seen a penny or a single toy."

Rose stroked Agatha's soft fur as Abigail rolled the dice.

"Swindling money from old ladies should be punishable by death," Betty declared.

"Betty!" Bridget's eyes widened. "What's all this talk of killing people?"

Betty just grunted and helped herself to another lemon bar.

Abigail moved her piece and then twisted a strand of fair hair around her finger. "Tank's been upset because Mike keeps flirting with me, even while dating Megan."

"Oh, that's just Mike being Mike." Isabella waved her hand. "He flirts with everyone. Tank shouldn't take it personally."

"Well, death threats aside," Bridget said with a scandalized glance at Betty, "he parks that meat delivery truck of his in our loading zone for hours, even when he's just getting lunch-"

"Or flirting," Isabella added.

"Or whatever he's doing. Makes me haul bakery deliveries twice as far on foot."

Harrison set down his coffee mug. "He's costing the feed store business too, spreading rumors that the pet illnesses going around are from their food."

"Of course he is." Betty snorted. "He's a Cooper. Has to make sure everyone knows Cooper's Meat Processing isn't to blame."

Rose blinked, amazed at the flood of complaints about one person. Since moving to Whispering Pines only recently, she'd had the impression every got along pretty well. And Mike had seemed friendly enough when she'd stopped by

Enchanted Tails Pet Boutique to pick up Christie's food.

As the game and the gossip went on, her eyes kept drifting to Jack's empty chair. Why hadn't he come, or even texted?

When the games were put away and the last of the lemon bars and carrot sticks consumed, people gathered their coats, and Bridget paused by the newly hung frame.

"Are these your postcards?" She pointed to one. "That's from Old San Juan - where I grew up!"

"My mother sent them," Rose said quietly.

"Oh, does she travel a lot?"

"Umm…" Rose glanced at the cards. It had definitely not been a good idea to put them up. She wasn't ready to share this part of her past with her new friends quite yet. So instead of answering, she said, "I didn't know you were from Puerto Rico!"

Bridget talked about her mother and grandmother who were still there, and said she'd have to fill Rose in about some escapades over the summer involving her grandmother and a stolen painting.

Rose nodded, only half listening. It had been a fun- but surprisingly exhausting- night.

As she watched her new friends file out into the snowy night, she waved goodbye and agreed that they would do this again soon.

Then she closed the door with a quiet click, leaned against it, and wondered why Jack had never shown up.

Chapter 2

Rose straightened the display of romance novels near the front window, arranging them in a heart shape for Valentine's Day. The bell above the door chimed and her heart leaped - but it was just Mrs. Peterson coming in for her weekly mystery novel.

"Got anything new with cats solving crimes?" Mrs. Peterson adjusted her thick glasses.

"Three new ones just came in." Rose's eyes darted to the door as another customer entered. Still not Jack.

Throughout the morning, the shop filled with its usual parade of regulars. Mr. Chen browsed the travel section while his granddaughter played with Agatha in the children's corner. Sarah from the flower shop ducked in on her lunch break. The high school

English teacher, Mr. Roberts, spent an hour comparing editions of Shakespeare, and Kirsten Anderson from the elementary school stopped by to see about books to read aloud to her fourth graders.

Each time the bell rang, Rose looked up with hope that quickly faded. She kept checking her phone, but there were no messages from Jack.

"Everything okay?" Isabella asked as she paid for her latest Izi Miller novel- *My Very Own Hitman*. "You seem distracted."

"Just tired from game night," Rose said, though her gaze drifted to the door again as a young couple entered.

But she couldn't shake the hollow feeling in her chest each time the door opened and it wasn't Jack. She'd thought... well, she'd thought wrong, apparently. The invitation to game night had seemed like a natural next step after all their conversations. Maybe she'd misread him entirely. Maybe he was just a friendly small-town vet who talked to everyone the way he talked to her.

Rose taped the last paper heart to the bookstore window as the sun dipped low behind the pines. The evening light caught the glitter on the decorations, scattering tiny sparkles across the floor. She stepped back to admire her handiwork when a retching sound from behind the counter made her stomach drop.

"Christie?" She hurried around the display of romance novels.

Christie hunched on the hardwood floor, her cream-colored fur dulled in the fading light. A small puddle of vomit lay beside her.

"Oh sweetie, not again." Rose grabbed paper towels and cleaner from under the counter. As she wiped up the mess, Christie pressed against her leg, letting out a weak meow.

Rose scratched behind Christie's ears. "That's the third time today." Her fingers trembled as she tossed the soiled paper towels in the trash. Christie hadn't eaten since yesterday, and now she couldn't even keep water down.

Her cell phone sat on the counter, and Rose stared at it for a long moment. She'd been avoiding this call all day, but Christie's health came first. Taking a deep breath, she picked it up and dialed the vet clinic where Jack was the only veterinarian. She'd hoped he would reach out to her, but she couldn't let Christie suffer because she didn't want to be the first to call.

Her heart pounded as the phone rang once, twice-

"Whispering Pines Veterinary Clinic, this is Doctor Hilton."

Rose's throat tightened. "Hi Jack, it's Rose Bennett." Why did her voice have to come out so squeaky?

"Rose! How are you?" The warmth in his tone made her breath catch.

"I'm ok. But I'm worried about Christie. She's been vomiting since yesterday morning, and she won't eat." Rose walked around the cash register and paced across the shop. "I was hoping... do you have any ideas? Anything I might try?"

A pause. "Wow. Still not keeping anything down? Something is going around town." A pause. "Oh, I'm sorry, Rose. Can I put you on a brief hold?"

Before she could answer, the bell above the shop door chimed and Jack's voice faded into hold music. Rose looked up to see Mike Cooper- Megan's fiancé- stroll in, his expensive leather jacket catching the last rays of sunlight through the Valentine's decorations. He nodded at her and headed toward the nonfiction room.

Rose greeted him with a smile, her mind flashing to Betty's investment story and Bridget's complaints about the delivery truck. At least, she thought gratefully, Mike didn't appear to be intent on flirting with her.

She stuck her head in the nonfiction room, phone still to her ear. "Can I help you find anything?" The cheerful hold music grated on her nerves as she watched Mike pull out a book on finance and flip through it.

"I have a whole section on investments," she offered, "and will be getting a couple more titles in tomorrow. Let me know if there's something—I"

Mike opened his mouth to respond just as a voice cut through the hold music. "Hello? Who's calling for Dr. Hilton?"

"Um. I'm sorry. I was just talking to Dr. Hilton. This is Rose Bennett." She watched as Mike chose a book, took it to the main room of the store, and settled into one of the armchairs by the fireplace.

"And what's this regarding?"

Rose let out a sigh. "My cat, Christie, has been vomiting since yesterday morning."

"One moment please, let me tell Dr. Hilton."

"I already—"

The hold music returned. Rose glanced at Mike again. "Sorry about that. Were you looking for something in particular?"

Mike looked up from his book. "Yeah. Actually, I was hoping—"

"Rose? Dr. Hilton will be right with you," the assistant interrupted.

Rose held up a finger to Mike, asking him to wait a moment.

"He asked me to let you know he's just been pulled away for a moment."

"I was just wondering—"

Mike closed the book and stood, setting it on the edge of the fireplace. "Later," he said as he gave Rose a wave and a wink and headed for the door. The bell chimed again as he left, and Rose's shoulders slumped.

"I'm so sorry," the assistant's voice returned. "What were you wondering? We had an emergency come in. Could Dr. Hilton call you back? In the meantime, I'd recommend withholding food for twenty-four hours to let Christie's stomach settle."

Rose rolled her eyes to the ceiling. "Yes, that's fine. Thank you."

She set the phone down on the counter with more force than necessary. Not only had she gotten no new information about handling a sick cat, but she had also failed to find out why Jack missed game night, and lost a potential sale! She sighed and glanced at the finance section where Mike had been browsing, wondering what he'd been looking for.

Christie wound around her ankles, letting out a pitiful meow. Rose scooped her up, burying her face in the cat's soft fur. "I know, sweetie. I know."

Rose pulled back her comforter and slipped between the cool sheets. Christie let out another plaintive meow from the doorway.

"I'm sorry, sweetie. No dinner tonight." Rose patted the bed beside her. "Come cuddle instead?"

Christie padded across the room and jumped onto the bed, curling up against Rose's side. Agatha stretched out at the foot of the bed, her dinner apparently settling just fine.

Rose reached over to turn off her bedside lamp, leaving only the glow of moonlight filtering through her curtains. The familiar weight of Christie against her hip brought back memories of winter nights in St. Paul, curled up in her childhood bedroom while snow fell outside.

At this time of year, when they'd been getting ready for Valentine's Day, her mom would bring up hot chocolate for Rose to sip while they made homemade cards together. The marshmallows melted into sweet swirls on top as they'd spread construction paper, doilies, and glitter across Rose's desk, crafting elaborate valentines for her classmates. Her mom always said store-bought cards couldn't compare to handmade ones. When the valentines were finished and the scraps all cleaned up, her mother had read her a chapter from whatever book they were currently reading as Rose snuggled under her comforter, safe and warm and knowing she was loved.

Rose's throat tightened. The vintage bookshop her mom had run wasn't so different from Rose's own store now - warm, welcoming, and filled with treasures waiting to be discovered. She could still picture her mom carefully wrapping rare first editions in tissue paper, explaining to customers why each book was special.

That was one difference. Rose's bookstore carried current editions of easy-to-find books. Not rare first editions curated from expensive collections around the world. Putting her collection together didn't involve travel to exotic locations.

And unlike her mother, Rose wasn't hiding any secrets.

Christie's purr vibrated against Rose's side as she stroked the cat's soft fur. Tomorrow was Valentine's Day. The construction paper hearts she'd hung in the shop windows weren't quite as elaborate as the ones she'd made with her mom, but they brought some of the same warmth to the space, as well as that childhood feeling of being loved.

Rose pulled the comforter up to her chin. Would anyone think to send her a valentine? She pushed away thoughts of Jack - his missed game night, his unreturned call. Her mom would have known just what to say to make her feel better about it all.

Before.

Christie meowed again, softer this time, and Rose scratched behind her ears. "I know, baby. Tomorrow will be better."

Chapter 3

Sunlight streaked through Rose's kitchen window as she measured coffee grounds into her French press.

She opened her fridge and took out a tiny bit of boiled chicken, put it into Christie's bowl, and watched her cat devour it as if she were starving. Rose smiled at pet her. "Feeling better?"

Christie wound between her legs, letting out another plaintive meow.

"I know you're still hungry, sweet girl." Rose scratched under Christie's chin. "But that bit of boiled chicken is all for you this morning. I need to see how you do. I'm sorry."

Christie's blue eyes gazed up at her, and Rose's heart ached. She hated denying her cat food, even if it was for Christie's own good. At least Agatha was content, curled up on her favorite cushion after her breakfast made of fresh salmon. Agatha had always been a picky eater and required special food.

The kettle whistled. Rose poured steaming water over the grounds, watching the dark liquid swirl. She'd need the caffeine boost - Valentine's Day would almost certainly bring extra browsers into the store hoping to find the perfect romantic read.

Agatha followed her to the front door as Rose stepped onto the porch. The February air bit through her sweater. She pulled her key ring from her pocket and opened the mailbox mounted beside her door.

Her breath caught. Nestled among the usual bills and catalogs lay a red envelope. Rose's fingers felt awkward as she lifted it out. Her name was written in careful cursive across the front.

Back inside, she set her coffee down and slid her finger under the envelope's flap. The card was clearly handmade - pink paper framed a hand-cut heart made from deep red cardstock. Tiny silver glitter stars had been glued around the edges.

Rose's smile grew as she opened it. The inside was blank except for a short message: "Happy

Valentine's Day to someone who brings magic to Whispering Pines, one book at a time."

No signature. But the handwriting matched the envelope.

"What do you think, Agatha?" Rose held the card down for her cat to inspect. Agatha sniffed at it before batting it with one paw. "You're right — let's not get carried away. There are more important things than mysterious valentines. Like opening the store!"

She flipped the sign on the door to 'Open,' her heart feeling suddenly light. She didn't know who had sent the valentine. But there was really only one person who might have. Only one person she had shown or sensed any romantic interest in since moving to town barely two months ago.

She realized she was smiling as she sipped her coffee. The thought that Jack might have sent it, might have spent time creating something just for her, made her cheeks warm.

She propped the valentine on her desk, where sunlight would catch those tiny silver stars. Christie hopped up beside it, still seeking attention - and breakfast - while Rose sorted through the rest of her mail with a smile she couldn't quite suppress.

An hour later, Rose was ringing up a group of high school girls when the bell above the door chimed and Li Chen swept into The Literary Cat, her floral sweater bright against dark slacks. Rose looked up from arranging a display of romance novels on the front table.

"Good morning, Rose." Li's eyes crinkled at the corners. "I need a cookbook with Chinese dessert recipes. My granddaughter wants to learn how to make almond cookies."

"Of course." Rose stepped around the counter. "I have a few options in the cooking section."

As they walked toward the back shelves, Li paused at Rose's desk. "Oh! What a lovely valentine." She picked up the handmade card, turning it to catch the light. "The glitter is such a nice touch."

"Thank you." Rose's cheeks warmed. "Someone left it in my mailbox this morning."

"How interesting." Li set the card back down. "We received one just like it at the tea shop. Same pink paper, same little silver stars." She tapped a perfectly manicured nail against the desk. "Though ours mentioned bringing warmth to the community through tea."

Rose's stomach dropped. "Oh." She tried to keep her voice neutral. "What a... coincidence."

"Perhaps someone is spreading Valentine's cheer throughout Main Street!" Li followed Rose to the cookbook section.

"Yes. Maybe." Rose pulled out a thick volume titled "Traditional Chinese Desserts." Her earlier flutter of excitement about the valentine faltered.

"This one has an entire chapter on cookies." Rose handed the cookbook to Li, pushing away her disappointment. "Including three different almond cookie recipes."

Li flipped through the pages. "Perfect. My granddaughter will be so excited."

As Rose rang up Li's purchase, she glanced at the valentine still propped on her desk. The silver stars didn't seem to sparkle quite as brightly now. But she forced a smile as she handed Li her receipt.

"Happy Valentine's Day," Li called over her shoulder as she left.

"You too." Rose watched through the window as Li crossed the short distance to Time for Tea. The red and blue Victorian looked particularly cheerful today, with paper hearts decorating its bay window.

Christie wound around Rose's ankles, still hoping for more breakfast. Rose scooped her up, burying her face in the cat's soft fur.

"Who knows. Maybe silver stars were the only glitter available in the store. Maybe it's just a coincidence."

The bells at the town hall clocktower chimed noon just as Rose finished helping Wilma Olson select a mystery novel. As Wilma left, the door stayed open an extra moment bringing in a gust of cold February air along with Izzy, Rose's librarian friend, who balanced two paper cups and a white bakery bag.

"I come bearing gifts." Izzy set everything on the counter. "Emma's cinnamon rolls and coffee from Northern Pines."

Rose inhaled the sweet, spicy aroma. "You're a lifesaver. I was just thinking about lunch."

"I figured you might be hungry." Izzy unwrapped the still-warm rolls. Her gaze landed on the valentine propped against Rose's desk lamp. "Oh, how pretty! We got one just like that at the library this morning."

Rose's fingers stilled on the coffee cup lid. "You did?"

"Mmhmm. Actually, it seems like every business in town got one. The bank, the hardware store, even the gas station." Izzy broke off a piece of cinnamon roll. "Someone's been busy spreading Valentine's cheer. I'm betting on the elementary school. I checked out a stack of books on how to make valentines to several of the teachers."

"Right." Rose took a sip of coffee to hide her face. The warmth that had bloomed in her chest this morning at finding the valentine now withered completely. "How thoughtful of them."

Izzy wandered toward the stairs leading to Rose's apartment, where the door stood partially open. "Hey, are those new? The framed postcards in your kitchen?"

"Oh." Rose followed her gaze. "I just put them up a couple of days ago. They're from my mom, from when she used to travel."

"Really? Where did she go?"

"All over." Rose picked at her cinnamon roll. "She collected rare books for her shop. Paris, London, Istanbul... anywhere there might be something special."

Izzy's eyes widened. "Your mom was a rare book collector? That's amazing! No wonder you went into the book business. Did she-"

"Would you like me to make more coffee?" Rose cut in. "This is getting a little cold."

"Oh. Sure, thanks." Izzy gave her a curious look but didn't press further.

Rose busied herself with clearing away the empty bakery bag, grateful when Izzy steered the conversation toward the upcoming winter festival instead. The valentine was disappointing enough. She didn't need to talk about her mom.

Rose organized the new releases display as Izzy gathered her things to head back to work. "Thank you," Rose said with a quick hug. "The cinnamon rolls were amazing. You're an angel."

"An angel who's late getting back to the library!" Izzy laughed as she hurried out into the cold.

Rose scooped up Agatha and snuggled her face into the cat's side. "It's ok," she whispered. "It's ok if everyone in town got a matching valentine. At least the kids at the school thought of us. And someone special will come along. You'll see."

Barely twenty minutes later, the bell above the door chimed again as Izzy burst back in, her face pale.

Rose set down the duster she was using to clean the high bookshelves.

"You won't believe what happened." Izzy gripped the counter. "Mike Cooper was found dead at Enchanted Tails this morning."

The duster clattered to the floor. "What?"

"They found him in the back room of the store. The paramedics think it was a seizure. Or maybe a heart attack." Izzy's voice dropped. "And Rose - he was holding one of those valentines." She motioned to the valentine beside the cash register. "Just like the ones we all got. There were conversation hearts scattered all over the floor around him."

Rose sank into her chair. "A heart attack on Valentine's Day?" The words felt wrong in her mouth. "That's like the world's worst pun."

"I know. It's awful." Izzy shook her head. "And poor Megan. First her dog, now this."

The image of Mike sitting by her fireplace yesterday flooded Rose's mind, and she turned to stare at the chair he'd been sitting in. He'd been right there, trying to talk to her while she was distracted on the phone with Jack's office. If she'd just hung up, taken the time to help him...

"He was here yesterday," Rose said softly. "I didn't even help him properly because I was on the phone."

"You couldn't have known."

But Rose's thoughts spiraled to Betty's angry words at game night: *Taking old ladies' money should be punishable by death.* She remembered Tank's frustration over Mike's flirting with Abigail, the way everyone had something negative to say about him. She remembered how he'd winked at her as he left- flirting again.

"It seems impossible," Rose said.

"Well," Izzy wrapped her arms around herself. "The whole town is in shock. Yes. But what I feel bad about is how no one had anything nice to say about him." She winced as she said it. "Makes me feel kind of guilty."

Rose stared at her own valentine, propped innocently against the lamp. Just like the one they'd found with Mike. Her chest tightened as she thought of Megan, losing both her beloved dog and her fiancé in the span of just a few days. And even worse, on Valentine's Day!

"Poor Megan," she whispered. Even as she said it, her mind flitted back to Betty's words. *Publishable by death.*

Chapter 4

Rose picked up her fallen duster, her fingers trembling slightly. The wood handle felt cold against her palm as she climbed back onto the step stool to finish cleaning the top shelves. The familiar scent of old books and lemon polish wrapped around her like a comforting blanket, but her heart remained heavy.

A soft thump drew her attention. Agatha had knocked the valentine off the counter and jumped down after it. She now batted it across the floor, her pale paws swiping at the red paper hearts. Rose watched her cat play, feeling no urge to rescue the card. What was the point in preserving it when every business in town had received an identical one? She'd been foolish to imagine it meant something special.

Her gaze drifted to the chair by the fireplace where Mike had sat yesterday. The books he'd been browsing still lay on the small table beside it, waiting to be reshelved. Rose set down her duster and walked over, picking up the slim volumes one by one.

"*Get Rich Quick: 50 Ways to Build Wealth Fast,*" she read aloud. "*The Six-Figure Side Hustle.*" The third book was titled, "*Start Your Million-Dollar Business Today.*"

The titles confirmed everything she'd heard at game night. Betty's lost investment in the premium dog toy scheme. Harrison's complaints about Mike spreading rumors to hurt the feed store's business. Even his delivery van that always seemed to be parked in the delivery zones spoke of someone more concerned about chasing quick money than thinking of others or putting in steady work.

But still.

Rose sank into the chair, running her fingers along the book spines. Had Megan known about his schemes? She tried to picture what Bridget had told her about quiet, methodical Megan, who cleaned teeth, shopped with coupons, and volunteered at the shelter where she'd adopted Mocha, supporting Mike's get-rich-quick dreams. The two of them seemed so different - like puzzle pieces from separate boxes. But of course, she didn't really know Megan. Maybe Megan was all about getting rich quick.

Agatha abandoned the valentine and trotted over, jumping into Rose's lap. Rose buried her fingers in the cat's soft fur. Agatha leaped off Rose's lap and pounced on something near her feet. The cat batted a small piece of paper across the hardwood floor, her lilac-tipped paw sending it skittering under the edge of Rose's chair.

Not wanting Agatha to eat paper- one sick cat was plenty- Rose bent down to retrieve it. It turned out to be nothing but a crumpled receipt. She smoothed it against her knee, wondering if it was one of hers or had fallen from one of Mike's books. Or perhaps it had been lying there by the trash can all along.

It wasn't from The Literary Cat. Rose's eyes quickly scanned it as her hand started to crumple it again. Scrawled across the top in messy handwriting were the letters "DST-UNSF." Below that were some calculations, numbers scratched out and rewritten. At the bottom was a note about someone named Al Rosa.

Rose was already beginning to ball up the paper again, but paused as the letterhead caught her attention.

Cooper's Meat Processing was printed in bold type across the top.

"Cooper's..." She ran her finger along the words with her fingertip. Hadn't someone mentioned at game night that Mike's family owned the meat processing plant? Betty or Harrison maybe?

She smoothed the wrinkled receipt out again, studying the cryptic notations. Should she give this to Megan? The thought of Mike's fiancée, already dealing with both Mocha's death and now Mike's, made Rose's chest tight. Would Megan want every last trace of Mike, even something as mundane as an old receipt he'd used as a bookmark?

Agatha head-butted Rose's ankle, purring. Rose reached down to scratch behind her ears while still staring at the paper. It seemed almost cruel to bother Megan with something so insignificant right now. And yet...if Megan did want it and Rose threw it away, wouldn't that be worse?

Her phone's sharp ring cut through her thoughts, making her jump. Agatha startled and darted under the chair.

Rose's heart skipped as Jack's name lit up her screen.

Chapter 5

Rose's hand trembled slightly as she swiped to answer. "Hello?"

"Rose? It's Jack."

Her heart fluttered and she mentally told herself to stop it. "Hey. How are you doing?"

"Good. Well, actually, really swamped. It's been crazy the last few days."

"I'm sorry to hear that." She smoothed the receipt and smiled, ready to hear what had kept him from coming to game night. "It sounds like you've had a lot going on."

He gave a grunt of assent and said, "I'm calling about Christie. How's she doing?"

Rose paused and she blinked. Christie? Of course he was calling about her cat. This was a business call. "She's fine." The words came out clipped. "I mean, I gave her a bit of boiled chicken this morning and she's kept it down."

"Oh." Jack paused. "You sound upset. I know I should have called back sooner-"

Rose didn't reply. She watched Agatha emerge from under the chair and brush against her leg. Christie was laying across the small couch opposite the fireplace, her tail flicking.

"I've been swamped with sick pets," Jack said. "But boiled chicken is good. We've traced the illnesses to a batch of contaminated food from Enchanted Tails." He let out a breath. "That's actually why I'm calling. You need to throw out any fresh pet food you got there recently. We're seeing cases of listeria. Has Agatha shown any symptoms?"

Rose scooped up the receipt before Agatha could pounce on the valentine again. "No, Agatha only eats that special salmon food. She's too picky for the regular fresh food." She tucked the paper into her pocket. "I still have some for Christie, though. I'm glad I didn't feed her that this morning. I'll definitely throw it out."

The bell above the shop door chimed. Charlie, a local architect who was expecting her first baby, walked in with her husband, Aidan, their hands intertwined.

"Look, Jack, I have customers. I need to go." Rose didn't try to keep the edge from her voice.

"Rose, wait, one more thing-"

"Thanks for letting me know about the food. Bye." She ended the call and plastered on a smile for Charlie and Aidan, trying to push down her disappointment. She wasn't going to lose another sale while being stuck on the phone.

Rose tucked her phone away as Charlie and Aidan approached the counter. Charlie's green eyes sparkled despite the shadows beneath them that showed her pregnancy-induced fatigue.

"How are you both doing?" Rose asked, her smile becoming more genuine as she saw them grin at each other.

"Happy Valentine's Day!" Charlie gave Rose a cheerful hug. "We're turning the guest room into a nursery," she said, running her hand over her barely visible bump. "I've got all these ideas swimming in my head."

"The architect in her can't help but redesign everything." Aidan squeezed his wife's shoulder. "We need books on sustainable materials and non-toxic paints."

"And maybe some pregnancy books?" Charlie twisted a strand of light brown hair around her finger. "The morning sickness is killing me, though lately I've actually managed to keep down dinner."

"We went to Bella's." Aidan grinned. "Charlie's been craving their gnocchi all week and Valentine's Day seemed like the perfect excuse."

"More like all month." Charlie wandered toward the parenting section. "The baby seems to love Italian food. Which works out perfectly since I helped redesign their restaurant last year. We get a small discount." She smiled at Rose.

Rose followed them. "The renovation books are this way. I just got in a great one specifically on eco-friendly nurseries."

"Perfect!" Charlie's face lit up. "And maybe some books on Italian cooking? Since apparently that's all I can stomach these days."

"Second aisle on the left." Rose pulled the nursery book from the shelf. "Though I hear pregnancy cravings can change overnight."

"Don't remind me." Charlie laughed. "Last week all I wanted was pickles. This week, anything pickle-adjacent makes me run for the bathroom."

Rose led them to the cookbook section, trying to focus on helping her customers rather than dwelling on Jack's call. "We have quite a selection on pregnancy and childbirth. Have you read 'What to Expect'? It's a classic."

"I've been reading everything I can get my hands on." Charlie's hand rested on her barely visible bump. "But Aidan needs to catch up."

"Hey, I downloaded that app you wanted." Aidan smiled as he squeezed her hand.

The bell above the shop door chimed again. "I'll be right back," Rose said, hurrying to the front.

Abigail and Kirsten stood by the counter, their cheeks pink from the cold. Kirsten unwound her bright blue scarf while Abigail shook snow from her hair.

"Kirsten!" Rose said. "Those valentines were so creative. Thank you."

Kirsten's brow furrowed. "Valentines?"

"The ones from the students at the school." When Kirsten still looked confused, Rose explained. "The ones all the businesses received? I thought the kids from school..."

"Oh. Do you mean the valentines that came to all the businesses?" Abigail said, and Rose nodded. To Kirsten she said, "Remember I showed you mine."

"Oh!" Kirsten said. "I heard everyone who had a business in town got one. That must have been quite a project. But no, it wasn't us. We just made cards for the kids to give to each other and to their families. Though that would have been a sweet project."

"But Izzy said…" Rose paused. What had Izzy said? "She said she checked out stacks of books on making valentines. And Megan mentioned helping at the school, so I figured—"

Kirsten shook her head. "Megan? The dental hygienist? We had a couple of room moms helping, but Megan wasn't there."

"Huh." Why would Megan lie about that? But it hardly mattered now, with everything else that had happened.

"Poor Megan," Kirsten said softly. "First her dog, now Mike."

"Speaking of Mike." Abigail lowered her voice. "I know it's terrible to speak ill of the dead, but Tank is actually relieved. At least Mike won't be hitting on me - or anyone else - anymore."

"He did have wandering eyes," Kirsten agreed.

"I heard his death might not have been from natural causes." Aidan's voice made them all jump. He'd emerged from the back room with Charlie. "We overheard at the restaurant that the police are treating it as a potential murder."

"Murder?" Rose stared at Aidan, shocked.

"That's right," Charlie said, her hand resting on her belly. "Detective Lindberg and Officer Jessie were at the table next to us at Bella's. Jessie mentioned something about poison being found at the scene."

"The paramedics thought it was a seizure at first," Aidan added. "Or maybe a heart attack. But Daniel said the evidence points to something more sinister."

"Did they say anything else?" Abigail asked, her fair hair falling forward as she leaned in closer.

Charlie shook her head. "They were speaking quietly, but I definitely heard Jessie say it wasn't natural causes. Daniel shushed her when he noticed us at the next table."

"Oh gosh. And here I was telling you all what Tank said about Mike," Abigail whispered.

Rose gulped. She'd only met Tank once and didn't know him at all. He was tall and muscular with tattoos on his biceps. Would he kill over something as small Mike flirting with Abigail? Then she thought about Betty's comment at game night about Mike deserving the death penalty for stealing her money. The words had seemed harsh then - now they felt chilling. If she remembered correctly, Betty had been involved in a murder of some sort previously.

"I can't believe it," Kirsten said.

Rose's thoughts flicked to those get-rich-quick books. Had Mike been involved in something dangerous? The receipt in her pocket felt like it was burning with her desire to get it out and examine it again.

Her heart pounded as she rang up books- first Kirsten's stack of Newbery winners she would read aloud to her students, and then Charlie's pregnancy books.

When she had bagged up everyone's books, her customers left, and a gust of cold wind blew in as they called good-bye.

Rose flipped the 'Open' sign to 'Closed' and locked the front door of The Literary Cat. She took out the receipt and smoothed it on the counter. Her eyes ran over that small slip of paper with its cryptic notations. What did they mean?

"Murder," she whispered.

Chapter 6

Rose's shoulders sagged as she climbed the stairs to her apartment, the weight of the day's revelations pressing down on her.

She dropped onto her sofa and pulled her favorite pink faux fur blanket around her, scooping first Christie and then Agatha onto her lap. A battered copy of *Pride and Prejudice* lay on the small table beside her. She'd been planning to read it tonight, but somehow she couldn't bring herself to open it.

"Come on," she said to her cats. "Let's get some dinner."

In the kitchen, she pulled out the chicken she'd boiled earlier. Christie wound between her legs, meowing plaintively.

"Just a tiny bit," Rose said, shredding a small portion onto a plate. "We need to make sure your tummy can handle it. But I'm so happy you haven't been sick today!" She put Agatha's food into her bowl and wandered out into the front of her home, into the bookstore.

The receipt lay on the counter next to the cash register where she'd placed it earlier, those mysterious letters - DST-UNSF - and the scrawled note about Al Rosa catching her eye again. She picked it up, and carried it into the kitchen, studying the Cooper's Meat Processing logo at the top. Christie was delicately nibbling the bit of chicken.

She heated up the left-over homemade chicken pot pie she'd made a couple of days ago and settled herself at the table enjoying the warm meal as snow fell gently outside.

A fluttering sound drew her attention to the kitchen floor where Agatha batted around a piece of the valentine that had brought such fleeting joy this morning. The red paper slid across the hardwood floor as Agatha pounced, her fluffy tail twitching with excitement.

Rose sank back into her favorite kitchen chair - the antique one with Christie's favorite cushion. What a Valentine's Day it had been. This morning she'd been consumed with thoughts of Jack, analyzing why he hadn't come to game night, wondering if he'd sent the valentine. Now those concerns seemed trivial.

Mike Cooper was dead. Murdered, if the police were right. And this receipt... Rose traced the hastily written notations with her finger. The calculations, the cryptic letters, that name - Al Rosa. Was it important? Or was she reading too much into a simple scrap of paper?

She thought of Megan, dealing with two devastating losses in only a few days. Rose had considered giving her the receipt, but now... If this could hold a clue in a murder investigation, it needed to go to the police.

Christie finished her small portion of chicken and looked up hopefully for more. "Sorry, sweetie. That's all for now." Rose scratched behind Christie's ears. "We need to make sure you're really better first."

Decision made, Rose stood and grabbed her coat. The police station wasn't far, and she could walk.

She needed to do this before it got too dark, and before she lost her nerve.

Rose pushed open the heavy glass doors of the police station, warmth and noise washing over her. The small lobby bustled with activity as officers rushed past, phones rang, and voices overlapped.

"I'm telling you, there are strange noises coming from my basement." Mrs. Olson's bright pink sweater stood out amid the sea of navy-blue uniforms. She gripped her oversized purse tight against her chest. "And this time I'm certain it's not raccoons."

Officer Chen spoke into his radio while juggling paperwork. "Copy that. Send another unit to Highway 61. That black ice by the stoplight is causing havoc."

Rose approached the front desk, receipt clutched in her coat pocket. "Excuse me, I need to speak to someone about Mike Cooper."

The desk sergeant barely glanced up from his computer. "Take a seat. We'll be with you shortly."

She settled into a chair beside an empty desk, watching the controlled chaos unfold. Two officers huddled over a map, discussing search patterns for someone lost in the Boundary Waters. The radio crackled with updates about the accident at the one stoplight in Whispering Pines. Glancing at the nameplate on the desk, Rose saw that it belonged to Officer Jessie Lindberg.

"Mrs. Olson, I promise we'll send someone to check your basement," Officer Chen said, "but right now we're stretched thin."

Rose's gaze drifted across Jessie Lindberg's desk. Stacks of papers. A stapler. A manila folder with the brown stain of something on the cover. Her eyes landed on a familiar splash of red and pink peeking out from under another folder and her breath caught. With a quick glance around the room to see that no one was watching, she shifted the folder off the pink paper. Another valentine, almost identical to the one that was almost certainly currently being shredded by Agatha back home. But this one was crumpled, its edges worn as if it had been clutched tight.

This must be the valentine Mike had been holding when they found him.

Rose glanced around again. Everyone remained focused on their tasks, talking, hurrying down halls, talking on radios and phones. With trembling fingers, she reached out and carefully opened the valentine, expecting to see a message similar to the one on her valentine.

But it wasn't.

She leaned forward to better read the message. "Noses are wet. Diamonds are blue. Who in this town wouldn't want to kill you?"

She jerked back, letting the valentine fall closed. Her hands felt contaminated from touching it. The cheerful red paper now seemed sinister.

She sat stiffly upright, blinking in the bright florescent lights. Wow. No wonder the police didn't think it was an accident.

She lifted a pen and used it to reach out and open the card, reading the words again.

Noses are wet. Was that because Mike worked at the pet store? Almost certainly. But what about diamonds being blue?

As Rose stared at the threatening valentine, the sound of voices from around the corner caught her attention.

"And Jessie, I need you to check with the jeweler, Al Rosa, over in Silver Pines," Detective Daniel Lindberg's voice carried from his office around the corner. "See if there was anything suspicious about the purchases Mike made recently."

"Right," Jessie said.

Rose pulled the crumpled receipt from her pocket. Her eyes fixed on the scribbled note - "Al Rosa."

She jumped to her feet, receipt clutched tight. But before she could take a step toward Daniel's office, the front doors of the station burst open. Two officers rushed in, their boots squeaking on the linoleum floor.

"Major accident on Highway 61," one called out. "Multiple vehicles involved. Black ice."

The station erupted into motion. Radios crackled to life. Officers grabbed coats and equipment.

"All available units respond," the desk sergeant announced. "Detective Lindberg, they need you out there too."

Daniel and Jessie emerged from his office, shrugging into their coats.

Mrs. Olson clutched her purse tighter as officers streamed past her chair. "But my basement-" she started.

"I'm so sorry, ma'am," Officer Chen said, already heading for the door. "We'll get to it as soon as we can."

Rose stepped forward, lifting the receipt. "Officer Lindberg, I found something you might want to—"

"I'm sorry, Ms. Bennett." Jessie paused, adjusting her police radio. "Things are crazy right now. Is this an emergency?"

When Rose hesitated, Jessie said, "I'll contact you as soon as I can, okay?"

Daniel was already out the door. Jessie gave Rose an apologetic smile before hurrying after her brother.

Rose watched through the glass doors as police vehicles peeled out of the parking lot, lights flashing against the dark February sky. She looked down at the receipt in her hand, then back at the valentine on Jessie's desk.

The desk sergeant's phone rang again, Mrs. Olson sighed heavily, and Rose dropped back into the chair, realizing she'd have to wait to share what she'd found.

Rose's key scraped in the lock of The Literary Cat's front door. The familiar jingle of the bell above welcomed her home as she stepped into the darkened shop. Streetlights cast long shadows through the front windows, making the bookshelves loom in the dark as she walked past them.

"Agatha? Christie?" She called softly as she climbed the stairs to her apartment.

Christie's pale form appeared at the top of the stairs, followed by a gentle meow. Rose's tension eased at the sight of her cat looking more energetic than she had in days as Christie padded down the stairs.

"There's my girl." Rose scooped Christie up, burying her face in the soft cream-colored fur. Christie's purr vibrated against her chest as she carried her downstairs into the kitchen. Agatha appeared and brushed lovingly against Rose's legs.

She pulled it out of her coat pocket, hung her coat in the closet, and smoothed the wrinkled paper against her kitchen counter. Those letters - DSP-UNSF - stared back at her, offering no answers.

Christie head-butted her hand, demanding attention. Rose scratched behind her ears, grateful for the warmth of her house after the biting February wind.

"At least you're feeling better." She set her keys beside the receipt. "Though I wish I knew what was going on in this town."

The framed postcards caught her eye, and she turned to examine them.

Paris. Puerto Rico. Istanbul.

Rose touched the edge of the frame, wondering for the millionth time where her mother was right now.

She changed into her flannel pajamas and slipped under her comforter. Christie curled up beside her while Agatha claimed her usual spot at the foot of the bed. The day's events swirled in her mind - the threatening valentine, Mike's death, Jack's phone call that explained nothing about why he'd missed game night.

"Some Valentine's Day," she murmured, reaching down to stroke Christie's fur. Her thoughts flitted between Jack, her mother, Mike's murder, handmade valentines, and the mysterious receipt as her eyes grew heavy and Christie's purring filled the quiet room.

She fell asleep to a dream that she was selling postcards to all the people in Whispering Pines, postcards with mysterious notes scribbled on the back-

DSP-UNSF. When the police asked her what it meant, she said she didn't know. How could she know?

It was a secret valentine.

Chapter 7

Sunlight streamed through The Literary Cat's kitchen windows as Rose spooned cat food into two ceramic bowls. Christie wound between her legs, meowing insistently while Agatha perched on the counter, watching with keen interest.

"Yes, yes, breakfast is coming." Rose set the bowls down. Christie dove in immediately. "Much better than yesterday, hmm?" Agatha took her usual dainty sniff to check that her food was acceptable before taking a tiny nibble.

"You're such a princess," Rose said with a smile. She poured herself a cup of coffee and settled at her large kitchen table with a bowl of oatmeal. The morning light caught the edges of her framed postcards, making them sparkle. She felt more optimistic today -

Christie was better, and she had a plan to share the receipt with Officer Lindberg.

After finishing her breakfast, Rose gathered the receipt from the counter and walked past the stairs into the bookstore. Christie and Agatha followed, their bells jingling as they trotted beside her. The valentine she'd received yesterday lay abandoned near the fireplace, and Agatha immediately pounced on it, batting it across the hardwood floor while Christie watched from beneath an armchair.

Rose lit a fire in the fireplace and was about to toss the valentine into it, but Agatha was having so much fun, she decided it could wait. Instead, she spread the receipt flat beside her cash register, studying those cryptic letters once more: DSP-UNSF. The scribbled note about Al Rosa seemed more significant now that she'd overheard the detective mentioning that name.

She pulled out her phone and dialed the police station. After several rings, Jessie's voicemail picked up.

You've reached Officer Lindberg. Please leave a message.
BEEP

"Hi Officer Lindberg, this is Rose Bennett from The Literary Cat. I was in yesterday evening but missed you with all the emergencies happening. I have something that might be relevant to Mike Cooper's death - probably nothing, but I thought you should take a look. I'll be in the shop all day if you'd like to stop by. Thanks."

Rose tucked her phone away and gathered an armload of children's books from the cheerful yellow room. The morning sun slanted through the front windows, perfect lighting for a new display. She'd been excited to feature some of the latest arrivals.

As she crossed to the front window, Agatha abandoned the valentine to chase a dust mote dancing in the sunbeam. Christie emerged from under the chair, settling down to methodically shred one corner of the pink paper with her teeth.

"At least someone's enjoying that valentine," Rose murmured, setting the stack of books on the window seat. She had time before opening to create something eye-catching.

She jumped up to grab her book stands and caught sight of the receipt. She paused and pulled it closer, squinting again at Mike's hurried scrawl. The numbers at the bottom formed a messy column - $4,250... $3,875... $2,100. Each had been crossed out and recalculated multiple times, as if he couldn't get the math quite right.

She traced her finger over the letters DSP-UNSF at the top. "Disposable UNICEF?" She shook her head. That made no sense. "Displaced..." Nothing came to mind that fit.

Agatha hopped onto the counter, sniffing at the paper. Rose absently stroked her cat's silky fur while staring at those letters. The sound of passing traffic filtered through the front windows as her mind churned through possibilities.

"Dispose unsafe?" The words slipped out in a whisper. Rose sat up straighter and stared at the letters. Dispose Unsafe might actually make sense if there was meat at the processing plant that was supposed to be disposed of. But what would the rest of it mean?

As she stared into the unfinished display window, her mind turned over possibilities.

Dispose- Unsafe. Dispose of unsafe meat.

She looked at Christie now batting a speck of pink paper across the hardwood floor. Unsafe meat... Sick pets... Mike trying to convince people the sick pets were the fault of a feed store...

Could Mike have taken contaminated meat from Cooper's Processing Plant - meat that was marked for disposal - and sold it to Enchanted Tails for their fresh pet food instead?

She looked again at the calculations. The numbers were substantial. Enough to help pay for an engagement ring from Al Rosa's jewelry store? The valentine's words echoed in her mind: *Noses are wet. Diamonds are blue...*

Her fingers drummed against the counter. If Mike had sold bad meat to the pet store, knowing it would make animals sick…

Someone could have found out. Someone whose pet got sick. Or someone who lost money investing in Mike's schemes, or-

A sharp bang on the front door made Rose jump. Agatha bolted off the counter, bell jingling as she darted under a nearby chair.

Rose's heart quickened from the surprise as she hurried to the door. Through the glass, she caught sight of Megan's pale face and bright pink cheeks, her blonde hair windblown.

"Megan! Good morning!"

"I'm so sorry to bother you before opening," Megan burst out as Rose unlocked the door. She rushed inside, bringing with her a gust of cold February air. "I know it's early, but I wanted to check if that travel guide came in?"

Rose blinked. With everything that had happened, she'd nearly forgotten about the book. "The Southeast Asia guide?"

"Yes." Megan pulled off her mittens. Rose noticed her bare ring finger, the slight indentation where her engagement ring had been just days ago.

"I... wasn't sure you'd still want it." Rose winced at her own words. "I mean, after everything-"

"I just need to get away." Megan's voice cracked and she shook her head as if trying to clear it. "So I changed my travel dates. My flight leaves in a few hours. I thought maybe if the book had come in..."

"Oh, Megan." Rose's chest ached with sympathy. "How are you holding up?"

Megan opened her mouth, but for a second, no words came out. She closed it again and looked around the bookstore. "Not great, actually. But I just... I can't stay here right now. Mike and I were supposed to go on our honeymoon, and I know it sounds crazy, but I need to take this trip. For myself. To try to..." She gestured vaguely. "To get away. To try to process everything." She looked down and brushed a bit of glittering snow from her mittens.

Rose's phone vibrated in her back pocket. She pulled it out, glimpsing Jack's name on the screen. Her heart did a little flip, but she hit ignore.

"It's not crazy at all," Rose said softly. "Let me get the book for you. Actually, I ordered a few, since I wasn't sure which one you'd want." As she went to grab them from the unpacked delivery box in the kitchen, she realized Megan had requested this book the night before Mike's death, likely around the same time someone had delivered that threatening valentine. She pushed the thought away, pulled the books out of the box and hurried back to the front of the store as her phone vibrated again.

Rose handed the travel guides to Megan, her fingers brushing the glossy covers, as her phone continued to buzz. Sighing, she pulled it out and was surprised to see Jack's name again.

"I'm so sorry, Megan, but I need to take this call. It's the vet. Let me know which one you'd like, and I'll ring you up."

Megan nodded, clutching the books to her chest before glancing at them. "Of course. Thank you for getting these in for me."

Rose slid her thumb over the phone to accept the call and slipped behind the checkout counter. "Hi Jack."

"Rose, hey! Thanks for picking up. I finally have a few minutes to talk and wanted to catch you before your store opened."

"Thanks for calling back." Rose watched as Megan flipped through the books, set one on the cash register counter, and paced over to stare out the shop's front window.

"How are your cats doing?" Jack's voice was warm, and Rose had to remind herself not to melt, that he'd stood her up.

"Christie's much better today." She picked up the book on the counter and wanted to ask whether this was the one Megan wanted, but Megan seemed miles away and didn't notice. Rose's gaze fell to the snow Megan had brushed from her mitten. The glitter she'd noticed wasn't sparkling snow- it looked like a tiny silver glitter star. "And Agatha never got sick at all, thankfully," she finished.

"That's good news." Jack paused. "I'm sorry things have been so crazy lately. I've never seen so many sick pets in one week. And then this morning, something even stranger happened. As soon as I got in, Detective Lindberg came by to check my drug supplies. He wanted to know if any gabapentin was missing."

Rose frowned. "That is odd. Why would he care about that?"

"Because that's what killed Mike Cooper."

With a quick intake of breath, Rose turned away from Megan, as if this could somehow shield the woman from more pain.

Jack's voice dropped lower. "They found a lethal dose in those candy hearts that came with his valentine. The only places in town that stock gabapentin are my office and the dental clinic. The police are checking both locations."

Rose's gaze snapped to Megan, who was now pacing in front of the fireplace. Hadn't Bridget said Megan worked at the dental clinic? "Oh," she whispered into the phone. "That's terrible."

Rose half-listened to Jack as she watched Megan perch on the edge of a chair in front of the fireplace, a travel guide clutched in her hands as her purse dropped onto the chair. Megan let out a shuddering breath as she stared into the flames.

"I'd love to stop by later today though," Jack was saying, but Rose barely heard him. Her mind was caught on one thought.

Megan worked at the dental clinic.

Agatha batted the valentine across the hardwood floor, pieces of red paper scattering. The cat had nearly shredded it beyond recognition. Rose's gaze followed the torn valentine, her eye catching on the star-shaped glitter glued around the edges, then darting to the star glitter Megan had brushed off her mitten.

"I- I need to go," Rose stammered into the phone. As she rushed to gather the tattered remains of the valentine, her eyes flicking to Megan and the travel guide.

"I'm so sorry, Megan. That was rude of me to take a call while you're waiting. I'd just been waiting for that call for a few days, with my cat being sick, he was the one who didn't make it to game night, and…" She realized she was babbling, her mind spinning with thoughts of gabapentin, star glitter, and poisoned valentines. She swept the remnants of her own valentine into the trash.

"Can you ring me up?" Megan asked, handing Rose the guidebook she'd been holding.

"Of course. Is this the one you want?"

As the two women walked to the cash register, Christie pawed at Megan's purse where it sat perched on the armchair. With one quick swipe, the cat's batting sent the purse tumbling. The contents spilled across the floor - lip gloss, keys, a dental clinic ID lanyard, and a handful of small, pastel candy hearts clattered against the wood.

Rose stopped, the travel guide clutched in her hand as the pieces in her mind tumbled into place like a macabre puzzle. Megan's dog dying just days ago. Betty's comment that if anyone hurt her dog, she would kill them. Megan's job at the dental clinic- one of two places in town that stocked gabapentin. The lie about making valentines at the elementary school. And now, star-shaped glitter on Megan's mitten and candy hearts like the one that poisoned Mike, here on her bookstore floor.

Betty's words from game night echoed in Rose's mind: "*That little dog was everything to her. She got her right after her mother passed away...*" and "*If anyone ever hurt my dog, I think I'd kill them.*"

Rose's gaze darted to the travel guide in her own hands and then to Megan's white-knuckled grip In the edge of the counter.

A last-minute trip to Southeast Asia. Far from American police and extradition treaties.

The receipt with its cryptic notes about contaminated meat lay in plain sight next to the register. DST-UNSF. *Destroy, Unsafe*. Had Mike inadvertently killed Megan's dog with contaminated meat?

Rose swallowed as she stared at the receipt for a moment, then looked up at the woman before her. If Mike had killed her dog, even accidentally, and Megan had discovered Mike's scheme to sell tainted meat from his family's plant as premium pet food - would she kill him?

Chapter 8

Rose's fingers trembled as she punched numbers into the cash register. "When did you say you were traveling?"

"I just told you. Today." Megan tapped her foot against the hardwood floor. "My flight leaves in a few hours."

"That's... quick." Rose fumbled with the drawer, her fingers suddenly clumsy. Her eyes darted to her phone on the counter.

"With no dog here anymore, why wait?" Megan's voice cracked.

Rose nodded, her throat tight. No dog. But no mention of no fiancé. Her hand brushed against the receipt beside the register. She swept it into the cash drawer before Megan could spot it.

"Will you be gone long?" Rose's fingers inched toward her phone.

"It doesn't matter." Megan shifted her weight, checking her watch. "I don't think anything really matters anymore."

Rose picked up her phone, angling the screen away. Her thumbs moved across the keyboard as she texted Jessie. "Come now. Emergency."

"The weather there must be nice this time of year." Rose's voice came out shaky.

"Look, I really need to get going." Megan's jaw clenched. "I'm not missing this flight. Are you going to ring me up or should I buy a travel guide somewhere else?"

Rose hit send on the text to Jessie, her palms clammy as she picked up the travel guide.

"Of course. One last thing." Rose scanned the barcode as slowly as she dared, willing time to slow down. "Did you make those valentines? The ones all the businesses got?"

Megan became still and she stared at Rose. For a moment, the only sound was the whir of the receipt printer as the two women looked at each other. Then

Megan's voice cut through the silence. "Are you accusing me of murder?"

"What? No, of course not!" Rose tried to laugh. "I just wondered about the valentines."

Megan's eyes blazed. "You have no idea what it's like. No idea what it's like to love someone, to trust them, and the find out they aren't who you think they are."

Rose's mouth hung open for one second. She blinked in surprise and then glanced toward her kitchen doorway. The edge of her framed postcards was barely visible.

"Actually." Rose's voice softened. "I do know."

"You?" Megan's laugh was sharp. "You run a bookstore! You have a perfect little life! How could you possibly understand?"

"You don't know—"

"Of course I know." Megan began scooping up the things that had tumbled out of her purse, shoving them back inside pell-mell. "I lost Mike long before he died. Every woman in town caught his eye. Every get-rich-quick scheme meant more to him than me or our future together." Her voice cracked. "He even put

Mocha at risk. Knowing what he was doing! And for what? Money!"

Megan stood, her purse contents a jumble, and pointed to her bare ring finger. "That stupid ring. You know what? It wasn't even real. A fake diamond. He swore it was genuine." Her voice became hard. "And do you know how he paid for it?"

Rose whispered, "With contaminated meat?"

Rose's words caught Megan off guard. Her face drained of color. "How did you-" She narrowed her eyes at Rose and then waved a hand toward the travel guide. "You know what? I don't need to know. Keep the book." Megan backed toward the door. "I don't want it. I'm getting out of here."

She spun around as the shop door swung open.

Detective Daniel Lindberg stood in the doorway, Officer Jessie at his side.

Megan collapsed into tears.

Chapter 9

Rose turned the key in the lock of The Literary Cat's front door, listening to the familiar click, and then turned the sign in the window to 'Closed.' She looked outside. The setting sun cast long shadows across Main Street, and a light dusting of snow had begun to fall.

Agatha wound between her legs as she made her final rounds through the shop. Christie watched from her perch on the counter, looking healthier than she had in weeks. Rose scratched under Christie's chin, grateful that her cat had recovered from the contaminated pet food.

"At least something good came from all this," Rose murmured, straightening a stack of books. The investigation had revealed Mike's scheme of selling tainted meat to pet food manufacturers. The recall had saved countless other pets from getting sick.

She paused by the fireplace where Mike had sat just days ago, leafing through get-rich-quick books. The memory of finding that receipt still made her stomach clench. If she hadn't noticed those scribbled notes about Al Rosa, seen the glitter in the snow, and if Christie hadn't spilled Megan's purse contents ...

Earlier that day, Jessie had stopped by with an update. "Megan confessed to everything," she'd told Rose. "About discovering Mike was selling contaminated meat, about making all those valentines to hide the poisoned one. Apparently killing her dog had been the last straw."

Rose moved to the children's section, remembering how Megan had lied about being at the elementary school. Though as it turned out, she hadn't completely lied - she *had* borrowed a book about making valentines from one of the teachers. She hadn't wanted to leave evidence by checking it out of the library herself.

The cats followed Rose as she made her way into the kitchen. She thought about Megan's words that day: "*You have no idea what it's like to love someone who isn't who you think they are.*"

But Rose did know. Her eyes drifted to the framed postcards - her mother's promises scattered across the world. She understood all too well how it felt to discover someone you loved wasn't who you thought they were.

Rose filled the cats' food bowls, watching them eat with healthy appetites- Christie diving in, Agatha sniffing carefully first. The sound of their purring filled the quiet kitchen. Outside her window, the snow continued to fall, covering Whispering Pines in a fresh blanket of white, offering the town a new start.

The knocker's sharp rap echoed surprised her. Rose looked up from where she'd been watching the snow, her heart skipping as she recognized Jack's silhouette through the frosted glass.

She opened the door, and Jack stood there with snowflakes dusting his brown hair. "Hey." He smiled and her heart did a little flip. "I wanted to check on Christie and Agatha."

Rose stepped back to let him in. "Well, Christie's back to normal, and Agatha never got sick." She raised an eyebrow and gave him a half smile. "But you already knew that from our phone call." She closed the door behind him.

Jack ran a hand through his hair, dislodging the snow. "Yeah, I did." He shifted his weight. "I also wanted to explain about game night. I had an emergency call - a dog that had gotten into the contaminated food. I should have texted, but everything happened so fast."

The knot that Rose hadn't even known had been in her chest for days loosened. She'd been silly to be upset without knowing the full story.

"Maybe we could reschedule?" Jack's eyes crinkled at the corners. "Just the two of us?"

"I'd like that." Rose glanced toward her kitchen. "Actually, if you're free now, I picked up some chicken noodle soup from Mrs. Chen's shop. And Emma brought over chocolate raspberry cupcakes to thank me for helping with the case."

"Oh my gosh. Really? That sounds perfect."

As he settled at Rose's kitchen table, Jack's gaze drifted to the framed postcards on the wall. "Are these places you've visited?"

Rose stirred her soup, considering how much to share. The postcards were such a personal part of her past, but maybe it was time to open up. At least a bit.

"They're from my mother," she said. "She dealt in rare books. She traveled all over the world to find them, and she sent me postcards from everywhere she went."

"Wow. That's cool. And what does she do now?"

Rose set down her spoon. "I don't know. She disappeared twelve years ago. Just... vanished." She stared into the pot of soup. "Turns out, apparently she wasn't who I thought she was."

She ladled soup into two large bowls and set them on the table before settling into a chair beside Jack.

Jack tipped his head, studying the postcards before turning back to Rose. "You know what I think?"

She shook her head. "What do you think?"

"You've solved two murders since coming to Whispering Pines. Maybe you'll solve that mystery too."

Rose considered this for a moment, then relaxed into a smile. "You know what I think?"

It was Jack's turn to shake his head. "But I would like to."

"I think you might be right. Maybe I will."

Christie wound around Rose's ankles as Agatha jumped onto the empty chair, purring. Through the kitchen window, snow continued to fall on the quiet town. Rose looked from the postcards, feeling the familiar ache of missing her mother, to Jack who was sipping soup from his spoon and somehow managing to smile at her at the same time.

For the first time since moving to Whispering Pines, she felt like she was home.

Rose's Recommendations

Welcome to The Literary Cat where Rose is always happy to recommend a good book.

You might have noticed Isabella, who loves romantic comedies, checking out one of Rose's recommendations- Izi Miller's book, *My Very Own Hitman*.

This fun romantic comedy will sweep you off your feet with action, adventure, suspense and romance. Both the paperback and Kindle editions include access to a PDF with easy book club ideas and simple recipes to match the romantic dinner in the book!

You can check it out too! Just scan the QR code below!

Read all Penelope Loveletter's Books!

www.Penelope Loveletter.com

lots of love,

Penelope

LOVELETTER
PUBLICATIONS
EST. 2023

Printed in Great Britain
by Amazon